# Dragon Smart

Published by Dave Burgess Consulting, Inc.
DaveBurgessConsulting.com
San Diego, CA

Paperback ISBN: 978-1-956306-61-3

Illustrations by Tommy Richmond
Design by Liz Schreiter
Edited and produced by Reading List Editorial
ReadingListEditorial.com

# DRAGON SMART

**Written by Tisha Richmond**
**Illustrated by Tommy Richmond**

Every day, Tommy the dragon went to school.
And every day, he listened and followed the rules.

He memorized many definitions
and facts. He did equations, too,
that he'd add and subtract.

But often when the questions came, Tommy feared his teacher would call his name.

His friends had answers when the teacher would ask,
but Tommy's answers didn't come nearly as fast.

He wished and prayed with all his might
that he could learn without a fight.

He secretly hoped when he took a test
that he could, for once, score the best.

But when he'd get home and begin to play,
he'd forget all about his struggles that day.

Tommy drew pictures
and sculpted with clay.
Every now and then,
he'd help bake a souffle.

When it was time to go to bed, tons of ideas would swirl in his head.

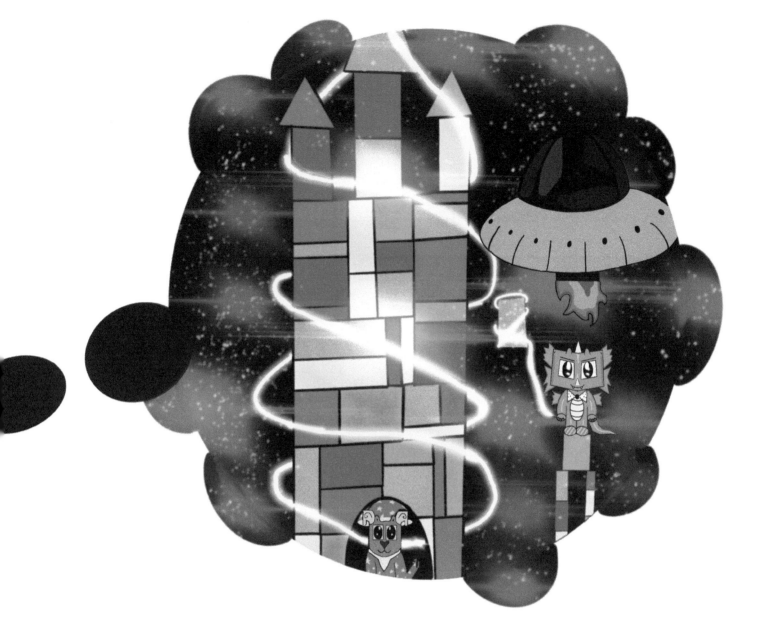

They'd dance and glide and whirl around, until
Tommy drifted to sleep, safe and sound.

But then, without fail, on the day of a test, Tommy would feel nervous as he got up and dressed.

Later, in class, when the test was passed out, Tommy would look at the questions and want to yell and shout.

All that he'd learned would swim in his head,
but it didn't connect in the way that he read.

The words would be jumbled and the numbers all blurred. The questions didn't fit anything he had heard.

Between the tick of the clock and the tap of a pen,
the sounds in the room would make his head spin.

He'd answer the questions and always do his best,
but Tommy had a feeling his test was a mess.

On one fretful test day, he'd had quite enough.
The questions on the test were especially tough.

"I guess I'm not smart," he said with a sigh and
released his emotions by starting to cry.

Tommy ran to his room when he got home,
hoping he could spend some time there alone.

His mom knocked at his door. "Are you feeling sad?" Tommy breathed fire because he felt mad.

"I want to be smart," his mom heard him say, "but learning is hard for me every day. I listen, I study, and I follow the rules, but no matter what I do, I don't do well in school."

His mom gave him a hug, looked him straight in the eye, and said, "You *are* smart, Tommy. Let me help you see why."

"You may struggle to read or count in your head, but you create fantastical stories all your own instead.

Your ideas inspire me with wonder and awe. You paint beautiful pictures we hang on the wall."

"Your heart can sense when your friends feel blue.
You invite lonely students to sit with your crew."

"You make everyone laugh. You are very funny
and make the rainiest days bright and sunny."

"You have a special sense of style and design clothes that make everyone smile.

You have rhythm and can keep a beat. You make all your friends want to tap and stomp their feet."

"My precious Tommy, I want you to know, you are one of the smartest I know.

You have a magic that is all your own. It will sparkle and shine even when you're all grown."

"Keep drawing and painting and sculpting and baking.
Keep listening and learning, and never stop making."

"Keep crafting jokes that make others smile, and keep celebrating your unique sense of style.

Keep dancing and dreaming and making your art. Keep showing others your big, caring heart."

"You are so special and loved beyond measure. Your smart is MAGIC, and you are a treasure."

**Tisha Richmond** is a Canva for Education Learning Consultant and Global Education Community Manager, innovative educational consultant, international speaker, podcast host, and author from Southern Oregon. She has served twenty-five years in public education as a Career and Technical Education teacher, district Tech Integration Specialist, and Student Engagement and PD Specialist. Additionally, she is the co-founder and president of a Southern Oregon CUE affiliate and serves on the executive board for CUE. Tisha is also the author of the book *Make Learning MAGICAL*, which unlocks seven keys to transform teaching and create unforgettable experiences in the classroom. Tisha is passionate about infusing joy, play, and gamified strategies to immerse and empower our twenty-first-century learners and make learning a MAGICAL experience for all!

**Tommy Richmond** is an Oregon native currently living in NYC. He is passionate about graphic design and illustration. He is excited to continue his pursuit in the design industry.

Printed in the USA
CPSIA information can be obtained
at www.ICGtesting.com
LVHW062006170124
769040LV00015B/601

Dragon Smart

Published by Dave Burgess Consulting, Inc.
DaveBurgessConsulting.com
San Diego, CA

Paperback ISBN: 978-1-956306-61-3

Illustrations by Tommy Richmond
Design by Liz Schreiter
Edited and produced by Reading List Editorial
ReadingListEditorial.com

# DRAGON SMART

Written by Tisha Richmond
Illustrated by Tommy Richmond

Every day, Tommy the dragon went to school.
And every day, he listened and followed the rules.

He memorized many definitions
and facts. He did equations, too,
that he'd add and subtract.

But often when the questions came, Tommy feared his teacher would call his name.

His friends had answers when the teacher would ask,
but Tommy's answers didn't come nearly as fast.

He wished and prayed with all his might
that he could learn without a fight.

He secretly hoped when he took a test
that he could, for once, score the best.

But when he'd get home and begin to play,
he'd forget all about his struggles that day.

Tommy drew pictures
and sculpted with clay.
Every now and then,
he'd help bake a souffle.

When it was time to go to bed, tons
of ideas would swirl in his head.

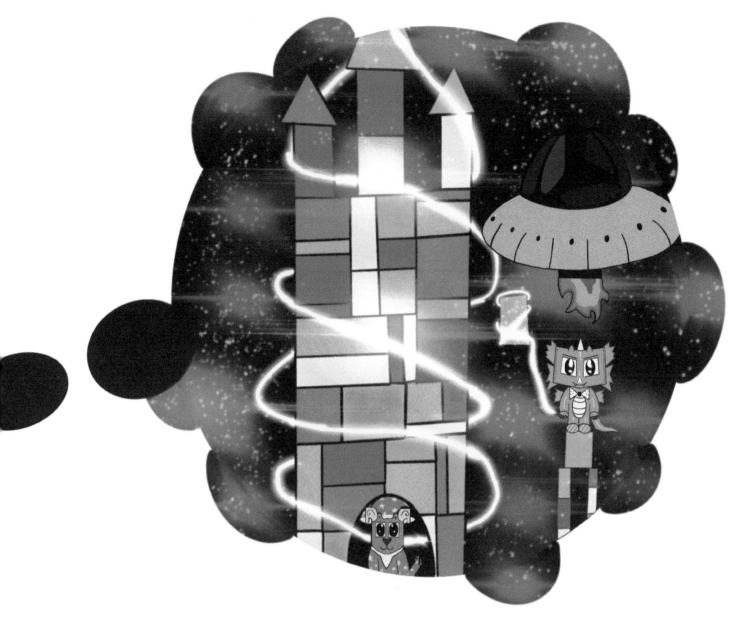

They'd dance and glide and whirl around, until
Tommy drifted to sleep, safe and sound.

But then, without fail, on the day of a test, Tommy would feel nervous as he got up and dressed.

Later, in class, when the test was passed out, Tommy would look at the questions and want to yell and shout.

All that he'd learned would swim in his head,
but it didn't connect in the way that he read.

RED

The words would be jumbled and the numbers all blurred. The questions didn't fit anything he had heard.

Between the tick of the clock and the tap of a pen,
the sounds in the room would make his head spin.

He'd answer the questions and always do his best,
but Tommy had a feeling his test was a mess.

On one fretful test day, he'd had quite enough.
The questions on the test were especially tough.

"I guess I'm not smart," he said with a sigh and
released his emotions by starting to cry.

Tommy ran to his room when he got home,
hoping he could spend some time there alone.

His mom knocked at his door. "Are you feeling sad?" Tommy breathed fire because he felt mad.

"I want to be smart," his mom heard him say, "but learning is hard for me every day. I listen, I study, and I follow the rules, but no matter what I do, I don't do well in school."

His mom gave him a hug, looked him straight in the eye, and said, "You *are* smart, Tommy. Let me help you see why."

"You may struggle to read or count in your head, but you create fantastical stories all your own instead.

Your ideas inspire me with wonder and awe. You paint beautiful pictures we hang on the wall."

"Your heart can sense when your friends feel blue.
You invite lonely students to sit with your crew."

"You make everyone laugh. You are very funny
and make the rainiest days bright and sunny."

"You have a special sense of style and design clothes that make everyone smile.

You have rhythm and can keep a beat. You make all your friends want to tap and stomp their feet."

"My precious Tommy, I want you to know, you are one of the smartest I know.

You have a magic that is all your own. It will sparkle and shine even when you're all grown."

"Keep drawing and painting and sculpting and baking.
Keep listening and learning, and never stop making."

"Keep crafting jokes that make others smile, and keep celebrating your unique sense of style.

Keep dancing and dreaming and making your art. Keep showing others your big, caring heart."

"You are so special and loved beyond measure. Your smart is MAGIC, and you are a treasure."

**Tisha Richmond** is a Canva for Education Learning Consultant and Global Education Community Manager, innovative educational consultant, international speaker, podcast host, and author from Southern Oregon. She has served twenty-five years in public education as a Career and Technical Education teacher, district Tech Integration Specialist, and Student Engagement and PD Specialist. Additionally, she is the co-founder and president of a Southern Oregon CUE affiliate and serves on the executive board for CUE. Tisha is also the author of the book *Make Learning MAGICAL*, which unlocks seven keys to transform teaching and create unforgettable experiences in the classroom. Tisha is passionate about infusing joy, play, and gamified strategies to immerse and empower our twenty-first-century learners and make learning a MAGICAL experience for all!

**Tommy Richmond** is an Oregon native currently living in NYC. He is passionate about graphic design and illustration. He is excited to continue his pursuit in the design industry.

Printed in the USA
CPSIA information can be obtained
at www.ICGtesting.com
LVHW062006170124
769040LV00015B/601

# TOOTSIE TAKES FIFTH

Written by
## Jano Stack

Illustrations by
## Jessica June Avrutin

## *ACKNOWLEDGEMENTS*

Pamela Dillman

Chrissy Waterman

Allie and Viki Baena (Pop Pop & Tootsie)

*for all the extraordinary moms everywhere*

# TOOTSIE TAKES FIFTH

written by
**Jano Stack**

illustrations by
*Jessica June Avrutin*

*It* was deep into November. The week after Thanksgiving in Connecticut, and my mother had been banging around the kitchen for days. From Stamford to Boston, the New Haven Railroad was packed with kids from every town going back to finish a few weeks and a few exams before coming home again for the Christmas break. My brother had even gone back to his boarding school in Massachusetts. Relatives and friends who had visited over Thanksgiving had returned home to exotic places like Baldwin, Long Island; or Harrison, New York, where my favorite cousins were from; or to Flemington, New Jersey (where they made fur coats and held the famous Lindberg kidnapping trial). The groups were all gone now. Groups that had come in shifts and waves, little clusters forming and dissolving into new little clusters which always seemed to me to be eating, drinking, and smoking cigarettes.

All of us children were not the main focus, thank God. It was the adults who were animated with the private thoughts and secrets that all grown-ups carry with them to holiday gatherings and family reunions.

But this was a happy time for everyone. It was 1960. I was only ten and nothing had really happened yet in my life. We children stayed out of the scrutiny of our parents. It was like that when so many of us outnumbered the adults. We had no nannies or housekeepers (except for my Aunt Julie who traveled with her maid Viki "even when business is bad," I heard my Uncle Bob say). We all, a dozen of us, watched out for each other. From baby Andrea, who my Aunt Ri said was a "mistake," to my cousin Val who was marrying her boyfriend Ted, who everyone said looked like Paul Newman in *Hud*.

If we were lucky it was already cold, and autumn had been rich and full, not humid and fickle with some days spring-like and others bitter. If we were lucky it was cold and the skies were bursting with snow and we had had fires going in the house since Halloween. We lived in New England and everyone started having fires October 1st. That's just the way we began to get cozy for the winter.

My mother's nickname was Tootsie, but only my father and her oldest friends called her that. My mother's Uncle Victor was Hungarian, and he'd always called her "my Little Tootsie." (We children were afraid of him. He was a jeweler in New York, with a mole on his lip, and freckles. It was scary for someone that old to have freckles.) There are several versions of how my mother, who never really struck us as a "Tootsie," got her name. The story I stick with is that as a spoiled, adorable, only child  with a head full of curls, she was indulged with Tootsie Rolls, a new candy, by her doting mother who bought them for her by the bagful. My mother had a passion for this candy that my father shared with her all their lives. Tootsie Rolls were part of our Sunday runs to Molly's candy store where we got the *New York Times*, and of course they were a favorite at the Capital Movie Theater in Port Chester where we saw *To Kill a Mockingbird* and used as bribes for long car rides to Cape Cod.

Tootsie changed her ensemble only once during the holiday, from a strand of pearls (Uncle Victor's find) with a caramel-colored cashmere sweater and a wool skirt and loafers, to a strand of pearls, sweater-and-skirt, and my Dad's fleece slippers, size 13D — his favorite Father's Day present from *LL Bean,* a catalog that carried items like that. Hard-to-find.

I can hear a sound even now when I think about it. You don't hear it much these days. It was when the lining of my mother's skirt rubbed against her nylon stockings. It makes me miss her.

*It* was deep into November, I was ten and my sister was eight.

Our house smelled of cloves and turkey, a smell that lingered for days until a new smell came along, of tangerines and shortbread, say. Our days began to fill with projects and more projects. It was to me the most magnificent and perfect time in the year. I think of that moment in a darkened theater when the violins are done tuning and the orchestra begins the overture and you squeeze the person next to you as the curtain rises. It was like that. When you grew up on the East Coast and autumn was finally

over, finally, with not even one leaf left on any tree in Greenwich, Connecticut, you felt a kind of anticipation, like something extraordinary was in the making, something was about to whoosh into your life — and any second now, Christmas would begin.

Tootsie underwent a transformation from our ordinary Mother who vacuumed with reading glasses and drove a station wagon, to the astonishing Tootsie, creator and director of the most perfect holiday of the year. She appeared almost translucent to us, with a light dusting of

powdered sugar, smelling of melted chocolate. The dining room table (with extra boards put in) and the kitchen table (large enough for six-man Monopoly) were both set up for the festivities. It forced us to have dinner at the counter and use those TV trays my mother tried to hide. We designed felt stocking with stenciled letters for our names and outlined Christmas cookie cutters for the shapes, and we sewed the sides up with yarn. We never bought Christmas cards from Meads, our local stationery store, like our friends; we always made them, out of everything from Victorian angels to mod gold mesh. We were the first to sign the daring "Merry Xmas" when we ran out of space on the card. I like to think that my sister and I were born with glue guns in our hands instead of rattles. We were babies brushed with Elmer's Glu-All and dipped in glitter like sugar cookies.

Tootsie was dazzling to us. She let us leave all the mess and never clean up. Day after day the projects stayed alive in mid-production: doll beds made out of cigar boxes and thread spools, Santa and Mrs. Claus Dewar's Scotch-bottle covers, wax snowflake candles squooshed and lopsided with little handprints. We made ornaments out of pipe-cleaners and ping pong balls. We learned how to pull taffy. We broke peanut brittle with my Dad's good hammer.

Even our most indifferent, savvy friends begged to come over. Our cousins were always invited, and invited to bring their friends. "You have to be able to get glitter in your hair and glue on your sweaters," we told them. Some had to borrow clothes from us. They had moms with perfectly still hair and really clean homes. We even had a friend, Kate, whose family had an artificial tree — which meant it wasn't real and didn't smell but the dried pine needles never dropped on the carpet and made a mess.

*It* was deep into November, the week after Thanksgiving.

And Tootsie came into our bedroom on a school night and sat down on the end of the big double bed my sister and I shared.

"Well, girls?" she asked us quietly. "Should we go into Town tomorrow and see the Windows?"

We did not move for a moment. And then we started kicking each other, wiggling up and down under the covers like human Slinkies. Tootsie smelled of Arpège by Lanvin and poached apples.

We never loved her as much as at this moment. Whispering on a school night. Forgiving her for putting us in bed now, a whole hour earlier. (Daylight Savings. When we got up for school at 7:30, latest, it was just getting light. And at 3:20 when we got out of school, it was just getting dark. I remember looking at our globe and wondering if this was what it was like to grow up in Iceland, or Norway.)

We, we three, were taking the train "into Town," tomorrow. During a normal boring Wednesday in Glenville School, we would be "in Town" when Miss Barker's Fifth Grade class divided into Religious Instruction for the Catholics and dodgeball for the Presbyterians. We would be in Town.

Tootsie talked softly to us as we abruptly stopped pinching and kicking. "We will take the train into Town and start at Lord & Taylor and work our way uptown and we will see how far we get." We would see how we "held up." She pushed her glasses up on her nose. And now we had to go to sleep or we wouldn't get to go. Period.

"Goodnight, my girls. Sweet Dreams. I love you."

I stared at the ceiling as my feet found the warm spot that my mother had just left. I thought about how Tootsie never called New York City "the City," like other people. She called it "Town." It was because she was born and raised there, and what was immense to some was small enough to her to be Town. We had been going to the Strand bookstore in

Greenwich Village since we were toddlers. And to BoBo's on Mott & Pell in Chinatown for dim sum, and Vincent's Clam Bar in Little Italy for cannolis. We knew the schedule for the Staten Island Ferry, and the best place to play hide-and-seek in the old Tavern on the Green in Central Park. We even knew about Phillipe, the *maître d'* at the Palm Court at the Plaza. (Eloise being one of the first books I ever sounded-out alone and read without help.) My mother divided the world into two groups: Those Who Knew New York City and those unfortunate souls who did not.

It was a week after Thanksgiving and I was dizzy, just thinking about trains and tomorrow and New York. I curled up around my sister, counted her breathing, and fell asleep.

*The* very next morning in the early gray cold we bundled up in layers of sweaters and our loden coats with the itchy collars. My sister and I argued over the least scratchy beret and kissed my Dad goodbye. The good thing about my father was that he, too, had grown up in New York City, and he'd known Tootsie since they were nine and twelve. Taking a day off from school to go into Town made perfect sense to him. Tootsie would later tell Dr. Ferdinand, our school Principal, that an education of New York City was just as important as his sixth period volcano experiment in science class. My Dad laughed when he repeated that to us. Probably Doc Ferdinand knew not to cross Tootsie. She could be really haughty on this subject.

We three huddled into the car and drove to the Greenwich train station. It was not as fast as going to the Port Chester station, but it was much prettier. It took fifty-seven minutes to get into Town on the train running alongside the Long Island Sound, with six stops before 125th Street. (That was in Harlem, which Tootsie pointed out was a beautiful neighborhood when she was a child. Well, we knew better than to question our tour guide.) We bought pretzels and ginger ale from the

bar-car, which smelled of old leather seats and Winston's cigarettes, and stood in the last car of the train, the caboose, facing backwards. It seemed important to see where we'd just been.

I don't remember what my sister said she thought about on those trips, hopping from the cold and excitement through a whole Town. But I know what I thought. These adventures were like being inside an enormous snow shaker or some other magical glass dome world. Taking a day off from school to see the Christmas windows was not like going to see the opening of the Guggenheim Museum, which had ramps instead of stairs, or even attending a Saturday matinee of Camelot, starring Julie Andrews, Robert Goulet, and Richard Burton (a cast "the like of which would never be on the stage together again," Tootsie sobbed as she dragged us ungrateful daughters away from our beloved *Sky King* and *Flicka, The Story of a Horse and The Boy Who Loved Him*).

Part of what I felt, I think, was wanting to love something as much as my mother did. So we could all be cast under the same spell.

*When* we arrived at Grand Central Station, Tootsie always said the same thing. "If you get lost, you wait under the Big Clock and never speak to anyone. I will find you. You have dimes." We said we knew, and Dad's office number was Ludlow 3-46-46. And off we strode in step past the Big Clock and out into a blast of cold air and the 42nd Street wind and chill that found its way up my sleeve like a frozen finger.

Here's what we liked: keeping a lookout for open subway grates and balancing our skinny selves on the metal railings, letting the steamy soupy draught curl up around our legs and bottoms. Oddly, this was not a sport that frightened my mother.

Here's what we didn't like: roasted chestnuts. They were yet another inexplicable thing that would become an acquired taste in our adul lives, like, say, artichokes, or arugula, o Ronald Reagan. We never told Tootsie we just pretended to peel the shells, dropping them slyly in the gutter on ou little procession.

My mother felt so tall to me then that it seemed like she bent in half to come down and speak to us face to face. "Okay." She would take us into the huddle. The coach and the players. "Let's start at the Library and go down to 34th, then we'll just see. Yes? Ready? Don't slouch," she answered herself. We two would push back our berets, which kept sliding over our eyes, and we'd hike up the crotches of our tights, which kept sliding down to our knees. Tootsie, the Commander in alligator pumps and matching bag. We pushed along 42nd Street. Snow flurries swirled up backwards from the sidewalk. We pushed along, chins high, mitten to glove, glove to mitten. Two little bookends, Tootsie in the middle.

Every time we passed any open department store doors, the most exotic aroma would smack us. It was the warm air of the whole cosmetic department, mingling with bus exhaust and people smells. Did everybody know that scent? I sure did.

Tootsie pointed to the two great lions in front of the New York Public Library. They were enormous, with stupendous Christmas wreaths around their necks. Everyone was taking pictures. Brownie cameras, Kodaks, and a new Polaroid called "The Swinger." ("It's more than a camera, it's almost alive! Only nineteen dollars and ninety-five" sang the girl on the commercial.) We were fascinated with all the photo-taking and goggling tourists. We did not bring our own Brownies along; we were not allowed. We were not Tourists, we were New Yorkers.

A few blocks past the Library was Kresge's Five and Dime where we sometimes bought M&Ms or a Jean Nate bath duo, or a Parker pen set for my brother. But not today. This was not a shopping trip. It was an expedition.

Tootsie looked intent after a few blocks, and passionate after a few more. My sister and I were already freezing. The clips holding our mittens on turned to ice and froze on our wrists. We did not complain. We pulled our sweaters down over our hands, and our arms became brightly-colored elephant trunks. Our berets were pulled so low that they almost touched our collars. Only our eyes were exposed.

"There! We'll start there." Tootsie was decisive. She pointed to the beginning of a long velvet rope. Men were ushering us into place: "Single file, one line, please." It was still morning, with not a lot of people. And because it was a school day, there were hardly any kids. Santas were ringing bells for the Salvation Army, which really was an army to help the poor. My sister asked me if Santa Claus wa born in New York City. I didn't know. But I remember the Santas looking like the real Santa in Miracle on 34th Street. Tootsie said that all Santas looked "jolly." And after all, this was only 1960 and probably all Santas still felt "jolly." My sister and I called everyone "jolly, jolly, jolly" that day until my mother said, "Please, girls, my ears are falling off."

*We* began at Lord & Taylor's department store, window by window. They had created miniature scenes of *A Christmas Carol* by Charles Dickens. We had seen and read many versions, but we were still not prepared for this display. Each window was framed with snow. I think it was Glass Wax, but I couldn't tell. Every character was splendid, dressed up in old-fashioned English costumes. We knew they were English because the signs said "Liverpool," and "Surrey," and "London, England." All of the characters were moving from side to side or taking their top hats off, men bowing to women, women curtseying back to men. There were big speakers, amplifiers that had Christmas carols playing, and the dolls — because that's what they really were — held hands in circles, holding their muffs (a coveted fashion accessory, even then) and wearing hoop skirts; and even though their mouths weren't moving, it seemed as though they were actually singing. In one box a circle of children was skating on a glass pond, chasing a small dog. We saw Scrooge carrying Tiny Tim on his shoulders, the best part of the story. All the while we three were moving slowly against the flurries and following the velvet rope. My little

sister was so overcome with music and the moment and probably hunger that she stood on tiptoe and pushed her beret back almost off her head. She began to hop, and leaned in as if to climb into the box and join the Ghost of Christmas Past. Maybe she was trying to eat the snow, because she started to lick the windowpane.

"Don't lick the window, Chrissy," said Tootsie quietly. "You just never know who's licked it before you."

Window after window of these mechanical people who decorated Christmas trees and threw their heads back and laughed, HaHaHa and real snow even fell in these boxes, everybody said

A man in a uniform looked at my sister and me and asked, "Why aren't you in school today?" Since it was a school day, lots of people looked at us, but really we could have been going to Dr. Gray, our dentist on Park Avenue, or Dr. Hochbaum for throats, ears, and nose on Lexington. I spoke for both of us when I answered boldly, "We came in to see the Windows." The doorman smiled approvingly at Tootsie, and now four of us were in on the most intimate of field trips.

We went window by window, moment by moment. We were never rushed, and Tootsie so transfixed herself that I got incredibly sad for a moment gazing at her and promised myself never to be mean to her again. This time I really meant it.

We knew that day that there were not many mothers like ours who believed that the Christmas windows at Saks Fifth Avenue and FAO Schwarz were as important to see as, say, the Mummies or the Primates exhibits at the Museum of Natural History or the Galaxy in the Star Theatre at the Planetarium. Tootsie was never actually conventional. ("Actually" being a new word my sister had just learned and used to start or end each sentence.)

We walked almost ten blocks because we wanted desperately to "hold up;" and Tootsie only walked in New York, saving a cab ride solely for the way home.

At Saks, each window was from The Nutcracker, which we had seen at Lincoln Center with a ballet dancer named Rudolf Nureyev — who wouldn't be a Russian anymore soon — and who made me cry when (I thought) he flew across the stage. With no wires. Frightened, I had hidden my head in Tootsie's shoulder. I would have done that with my father if he were there, but he never liked coming to the theater or the ballet, and certainly never to the Windows. He loved the Yankees, playing golf with his friend Dr. Welsh, and having a steak and vodka at the Saw Pit in Port Chester. He said he'd "had enough of New York to last a lifetime," and so with my brother not that enthralled either, it was our gift to each other, we three girls. We just loved everything about New York City. We saw it through the eyes and the heart of our mother, and it would become our Town too. A place we ran to for years to come.

*We* stopped for lunch, I think maybe at Horn & Hardart Automat, midtown. We ate there a lot. Tootsie said it was the essence of New York. always got macaroni and a hard roll, and milk; thirty-five cents and fifteen cents. You got exact change from the lady in the pretty cage-like booth. She wore clean white gloves.

We would move on toward Tiffany's, the most beautiful jewelry store in the world. (Not like Uncle Victor's. Uncle Victor had a dark jewelry store in a place on 47th Street called The Exchange.) We were never allowed in Tiffany's. Tootsie thought children should never be in three places: her living room, the grown-up side of a library, and Tiffany's. I can tell you that one year — maybe this one — the windows were almost too much to bear. Tiny toy mice were dressed up and sitting on piles of diamonds, miniature sleds of sapphires and ponds of pearls. We stood incredulous.

We were children who had not yet seen a lot of jewels (except on our Aunt Julie). Our mother wore only her wedding ring and her Timex. I think we understood why the store needed all the guards, even if they sported Santa hats. We saw the holsters and pointed at them, until my mother said to stop it, we were being obvious (one of her favorite words).

At Bonwit Teller next door, the windows were decorated for famous Broadway shows. One *The Sound of Music*; the next *Peter Pan*; the next *My Fair Lady*. Tootsie hummed all the songs and I don't even remember being embarrassed because she was so happy. I remember instead that my sister and I took time to play with the velvet rope, twisting it and rippling it, first to me, back to her. We were snake charmers. Our mother stood still with her purse clutched to her chest and her beret cocked to one side, and she hummed "*Oklahoma!*" to the tiny cowboy figures in the window. I know that my mother didn't speak for a whole day when Bonwit Teller went out of business. She wrapped all those lilac shopping bags in tissue, like baby albums, and put them in the cedar closet.

This day, maybe we wound up at FAO Schwarz, its old building, not the new. The bluster and cold would whip up Fifth Avenue, and maybe it was already getting dark, the days being so short now. There was nothing in the world that compared to FAO Schwarz toy store, not for us, anyway. We saved every penny for doll house furniture and still own our Steiff animal collections. Each year the windows topped the ones the year before. Lionel train sets traveling in circles around Madame Alexander dolls, all ablaze in colored lights and orchestral music. Windows of stuffed bears making toys in workshops. And moving! Everything was moving! Paws holding hammers, pounding in rhythm to the drums.

We didn't ask to go inside, though the lines were not even long and I think trumpets were playing. "*Hark, The Herald Angels Sing*" or "*The Little Drummer Boy.*"

We had to hurry, Tootsie would explain, if we wanted to make the last stop: Macy's at Herald Square. We would find a taxi cab. Tootsie stood off the curb with cars coming to within an inch of her, it seemed. She waved her purse and the taxi pulled over. Every time. Tootsie the native New Yorker and her two tiny out-of-towners. Big hand to little hand. We leaned together in the back seat all the way down 5th Avenue and across to 6th in the rattling cab, and when Macy's came into view it was as if

there was a great bonfire in the center of the city. Every window on every floor had its lights on, and was draped in wreaths and garlands. There were dozens of those jolly Santas ringing bells with buckets, and real Christmas carolers in clusters at every corner of the store. The windows each told a famous literary classic story.

We didn't know them all, but there were titles under each window that I read to my sister and Tootsie read to me. *A Tale of Two Cities* or *Tom Sawyer* or maybe *Oliver Twist*. Wide-eyed and silent, we pressed forward so close that our eyes squinted and burned from the light and everything went out of focus. We were that spellbound.

*It* was deep into November, and we were on the New Haven Local Railroad, heading home, stop by stop. The City that was a Town was getting smaller and smaller in the dark.

I think that sometimes I remember everything being bigger than it actually was. Don't you? The house I grew up in, my grade school, my grandfather. But not the Windows at Christmas; not this Town. And not Tootsie. This would be one of the only memories that was truly as big as I remembered.

I have carried with me this one magnificent reference point my whole life: a snowflake slipping down my collar, and twinkling lights and trumpets, and just us three on an ordinary day with our extraordinary mother. It was to me the most precious and hopeful and enduring moment that I would come to know much later in life as pure joy.

# TOOTSIE TAKES FIFTH

## Jano Stack

has been writing stories since she was in the third grade.

Until now they've all been kept in a hat box.

"Tootsie Takes Fifth" is the first one to escape.

She lives in Santa Barbara with her husband who is typing this ...

because she only writes in longhand.

# TOOTSIE TAKES FIFTH

## Jessica June Avrutin

studied art at Tufts University and The Museum School of Fine Art, Boston. She later moved to New York where she worked as a textile designer for Martha Stewart and got to experience the magic of Christmas in the city. Today she is a freelance designer, illustrator, and artist.

Printed in the USA
CPSIA information can be obtained
at www.ICGtesting.com
LVHW062006170124
769040LV00015B/602